Short Stories of God's Goodness

Short Stories of God's Goodness

Mike E. Robart

To order additional copies of this book, contact:
Xlibris Corporation
1-888-795-4274
www.Xlibris.com
Orders@Xlibris.com
85036

CONTENTS

This book contains several short stories that were written to better inform the readers about the goodness of our Creator. Many people believe in a higher power but have never read the Bible or any other book containing Gods promises to His children. We are all His children, whether you believe in God or not. We are all given a free will to choose which path we take in life, the decision is ours to make and I hope that some of the stories will touch people's hearts and get them started thinking on what will happen to us when we finally draw our last breaths here on Earth. There is a place called Heaven and some people who have had near death experiences have come back and testified to that fact, we can believe them if we choose to do so, or we can reject what they say as nonsense. I for one believe in Heaven and Hell, I was raised a Christian and I believe we will be rewarded for all the right choices we have made on this Earth. I believe that Jesus is the Son of God and that He came to Earth to suffer for our sins so that one day we can return to Heaven, a place of everlasting joy and peace. Each of you have to make up your own minds, I hope that the stories in this book will help you in some way to decide. Thank you in advance for taking the time to read it and I truly hope you will find joy and peace as you read the stories.

ROMANS 5 : 8

GOD SHOWED HIS GREAT LOVE FOR US BY SENDING HIS SON JESUS TO DIE FOR US WHILE WE WERE STILL SINNERS.

MARK 10 : 45

THE SON OF MAN DID NOT COME TO BE SERVED, BUT TO SERVE, AND TO GIVE HIS LIFE AS A RANSOM FOR MANY

WHAT I LEARNED FROM MY HEART ATTACK

You don't have to be working to have an attack of the heart,
You need to know the symptoms, and what to do when they start.
I tried denial, thinking this pain would go away,
But it only got worse and I knew it was here to stay.
So we called 9-1-1-, they were there in a short time,
After they had checked me out, their conclusion was the same as mine,
I was definitely having a heart attack, my life was in Gods hands,
I guess it wasn't my time to go, I hadn't finished all Gods plans.
I remember looking up and asking God, will I see Your face, Your way?
He answered me back with a still small voice, "Not today."
I had no fear of death, I was very much at peace, knowing He was there,
I had no regrets or sorrows, I didn't have a care.
I trusted my God He is always at my side, He leads me through my trials,
I can't ever remember when He wasn't with me, I've known Him since I
    was a child.
I am very thankful for all the prayers that were said, God must have heard
    them all,
He kept me here to finish my journey, and I pray I answer His call.
You never know what the future holds, but if you trust and obey,
He'll lead you down the path to Heaven, because only He knows the
    way!!!

THE CREATION

Imagine if you can, total darkness. That is all God had to begin with and from this He created everything that has ever came into existence or will ever come into existence in the future. He spoke and the universe came to be and is continuing to form, man will never be able to fully comprehend it's vastness. This is when He created light, up until then it was just a black void, a universe and day and night in just one day, not bad, but nothing is impossible with God.

On the second day He created the sky and formed the Earth. He created a dome which kept the water from the Earth and sky apart. On the third day He separated the waters on the earth so that land appeared and on this land He brought forth vegetation, every kind of plant and tree. The waters He had gathered were called oceans and seas, He saw that all things were good.

On the fourth day He created the sun to rule the day and moon to give light at night, these would mark the fixed times of the year and separate night and day.

On the fifth day He created the fish in the waters and the birds in the air, He saw that they were good and He gave them His blessing and they began to prosper and multiply.

On the sixth day He created the living creatures, animals of every kind. He also created something very special, you and me and all His children, He instilled in each of us part of Himself and He gave us all a free will, we could choose what we would do and who we would follow. This was Gods greatest creation and He commanded all things to be blessed and multiply.

On the seventh day God just sat back and relaxed, He looked upon His creation and all that had come to be, He blessed it all and said this is good. God placed man in a very special garden, but soon they would spoil all of

His plans, but He knew what was going to happen and He had a back up plan, because He knew what choices man was going to make and He knew how He would later send His own Son down to Earth to redeem them from all the sins that they would get themselves into. Jesus came to redeem all men who would acknowledge Him as Lord and Savior.

THE FLOOD

When God saw how evil all of His creation had gotten He regretted ever having made us, even though we were a part of God very few acted like it. God had a plan to destroy all of creation except for one family, that was Noah. He and his sons still gave God praise and tried very hard to follow His ways, so one day God came to Noah and told him to build an ark, He gave him instructions and said He would come back when Noah had it completed.

Noah had three sons and they each had a wife, so they began building the ark, when they had completed it God came back and told Noah to take two of every kind of animal and get on the boat, He was going to make it rain, He was going to flood the Earth and all living things. The people laughed at Noah and his family, but they didn't laugh long when the rains began to fall and the rivers started rising, they climbed the mountains, but they too were covered. Everything was destroyed but for the animals and Noah's family. For forty days and nights it rained, all dry land disappeared nothing was left on Earth, it became as empty as it was before God had created all things. This meant everything had a new beginning, but God knew it wouldn't be long and evil would raise it's ugly head once more.

As the rains stopped Noah sent out a raven, when it found no place to land it came back to the ark, then he sent out a dove, it too could find no place to perch so it came back, about a week later he sent out the dove and it came back with a small branch in its beak. Noah waited seven more days and he opened the doors on the ark and God spoke to him to go out and replenish the Earth. God made a covenant with Noah and placed a rainbow in the sky, whenever he looked up after a rain he would always remember the covenant that was made. God would never again cover the Earth with water!!!

THE HAPPY HOOKER

Alice was a friendly girl, maybe too friendly. She was married but sometimes she just liked to party and things happen at parties that you just don't want to write home about! So it was with Alice, she knew other men and everyone in town knew about it but her poor husband, seemed he lived a life like a turtle, he kept in his shell and didn't get out much.

One day as Alice was having one of her affairs some of the elders came in the house where she was and drug her out, they had planned to stone her, that was the punishment back in the old days for anyone caught in adultery. Just so happened they ran into this young Jew who called himself Jesus, he had a following of men, they were called disciples or apostles. It seemed the elders were jealous of Jesus and they wanted to trick Him, they knew he had a soft spot for people but they also knew that he was well aware of the Jewish laws that anyone caught in adultery was to be stoned so they asked Him what should be done, kind of put Him on the spot because if He said let her go it would be breaking the law and if He said go ahead and stone her it would look like He wasn't a very compassionate teacher. As we would put it today, He was between a rock and a hard place.

Jesus knew what was going on and that they were trying to trick Him, He leaned over and began to draw in the dirt, not sure what He was drawing but it gave Him time to come up with a logical solution. He looked up at the crowd, they were all holding rocks in their hands, He simply said, "Let him who is without sin cast the first stone." He knew that they too had all sinned at one time or another in their life! As the rocks began falling to the ground the people left and Alice upon seeing everyone leave felt very relieved because she knew her life was in Jesus' hands, how He came up with this clever plan no one knew. Jesus looks up at Alice and said, "Isn't there any who can accuse you?" Alice said, no one sir, and Jesus said go your way and sin no more!

Jesus didn't come to Earth to condemn his children, He came to show us how we are to treat each other and forgiveness is a very big part of our lives, we all need forgiveness at times because we all make mistakes. To error is human, to forgive is divine. How much better this world would be if everyone just followed that rule. You will never forgive anyone more than what Jesus has forgiven you!!!

WHEN YOU ARE DOWN TO NOTHING, GOD IS UP TO SOMETHING

When you have lost your will to live and no one seems to care,
God reminds you He is love, and He is always there.
When your world falls apart, seems like everyone has said goodbye,
God is there to take your hand, to wipe away the tears you cry.
Your heart is broken, all hope is gone, I have nothing left to give,
God is there to pick you up, give you a reason to live.
When you are on the very bottom, it seems like there is no way out,
God can pick up the broken pieces and take away your doubt.
But you have to open up to Him, invite Him in your heart,
Give to Him all your pain and sorrows, make a brand new start.
Only you can invite Him in, what other choices can you make,
God has so much in store for you, but the first step you must take.
Ask Jesus to come inside your heart, let Him have control,
He will take your pain and sorrow, give you a brand new goal.
When you are down to nothing and everything you have tried has failed,
Isn't it time to turn to Jesus and let His love prevail.
He is there just waiting, knocking at your door,
But only you can open it, He is the Way, I am sure!
God is always up to something, He always wants our best,
Give your pain and sorrow to Him, He will do the rest!!!

PHILIPIANS 3 : 10-11

I WANT TO KNOW CHRIST AND THE POWER THAT RAISED HIM FROM THE DEAD; THEN I HAVE HOPE THAT I MYSELF WILL BE RAISED FROM THE DEAD.

1 JOHN 1:9

IF WE CONFESS OUR SINS, HE WILL FORGIVE OUR SINS, BECAUSE WE CAN TRUST GOD TO DO WHAT IS RIGHT!

THE LIAR

Satan is a liar. He is also a deceiver, he twists the truths to make us doubt. He has only one goal in mind and that is to try and steal everyone who was ever created from the family of God and he will use any means, even coming as an angel of light. God makes each human being and instills in them a part of Himself, but He also gives us all a free will. We can choose to follow His ways or we can choose to go our own way. Satan is always around trying to deceive us, for some it comes easy but for others there is no turning our heads from our Creator because we truly love God and we know He holds our future in His hands and He only wants the very best for us.

Satan was once a mighty Angel, he had only one problem, he thought he was greater than God, the One who created him in the first place. Satan thought if he could get enough other angels to follow him he could take over Heaven and do away with his creator and become ruler, little did he know that God was one step ahead of him because God is all knowing. He was banished from heaven although he still comes back to accuse Gods children, but God had a plan when he created man and Jesus, His Son, came to Earth to fulfill that plan, to suffer for all mankind's sin and all we have to do is be sorry for our sins and accept Jesus as our Savior, not a bad plan for us.

Satan kind of reminds me of a story I heard once, it was about this young girl who was walking along one cold day and she came upon a snake lying in a path, the snake was very cold and could not move, he asked the girl to pick him up and put him in her coat to warm him up. The girl said I can't do that, you are a snake and you will bite me and I might die, the snake answered back. I promise you I will not bite you, I just want to get warm. So the girl reached down and picked up the snake and placed him inside her coat, as he began to get warm he began to move around. She felt a sharp pain and realized the snake had bitten her. As she lay there dying she told the snake that he had promised not to bite her and the snakes only response was, YOU KNEW I WAS A SNAKE WHEN YOU PICKED ME UP! Satan is much the same, he will try to deceive you in any way he can, never let down your guard and always be aware, SATAN IS A LIAR, nothing will change him no matter what he tries to tell us!!

FROM RAGS TO RICHES

Let me tell you about Joe, he was born into a family of twelve, he was the favorite so he was always getting a lot of attention. This made the rest of his brothers mad, and he was kind of cocky, he kept having these dreams and in them his brothers were always bowing down to him, I guess you could call him a dreamer.

One day when his brothers were out watching the sheep he came and he was wearing a new coat of many colors that his father had made for him, they didn't like the way he was always being treated special!

So his brothers came up with a plan to kill him, some of his brothers objected to this, they new of an old well and they wanted to just drop him in there, finally they agreed to do this, after all, he was their brother. Later that day a caravan of merchants came by and they came up with this idea to sell Joe to the merchants and then they would fake his death. They would take his new coat and put some sheep blood on it and tell their father that Joe had an accident, some wild beasts must have drug him away and all they could find was his coat, so that is what they did, Joe's father was heartbroken since he was his favorite son.

Joe was taken to Egypt and sold as a slave to one of the kings top men and Joe proved to be a very helpful servant and everything that he did prospered for his master. One day when his master was out of town his wife tried to have a fling with Joe, but Joe would have none of that, she was drawn to this attractive young boy but Joe knew this was not right and he feared God so he ran away. When the master came back his wife told him how Joe had tried to seduce her and he had Joe thrown in jail.

While he was in prison he was given a task of running the prison and everything went well for him, he would still have dreams and he would even be able to interpret dreams of others in the prison. God was working in Joe's life all along and he always found favor where ever he went. A few years later the king kept having this dream and no one could figure it out, so one of the men who was in prison with Joe remembered how he could tell everyone about their dreams, so he told the king about Joe and Joe was sent for, he told the king that it meant Egypt was going to have seven years of plenty followed by seven years of famine. The king was so impressed with Joe that he made him second in command of all of Egypt and gave him authority to do whatever was needed to see that Egypt would not run out of food, so they built storage houses and filled them during the next seven years. Then came the famine and all the land around Egypt began to starve, Joe's dad and brothers heard there was still food in Egypt, so some of the brothers went there to buy grain so they would not also starve.

Joe recognized them as soon as they came in the court but his brothers did not recognize Joe because now Joe was dressing like an Egyptian and was in a place of authority, he had a plan to keep one of the brothers to make his father come to Egypt. He had a servant hide a gold goblet in one of their sacks of grain and after they left he had the army go out and find the goblet and arrest his brother, he knew this would not go well with his father and that he would come and try to save his son. While the other brothers were going back home Joe revealed himself to the brother who had been arrested and told him of his plan. When Jake heard what had happened he set out to Egypt to try and rescue his son and Joe's plan was right on course, soon they were all together, living as a family in Egypt. They prospered and the tribe grew in strength and number.

Joe had many trials in his life but God got him through them all. God has each one of our lives planned out to if we will just trust Him and try to follow His ways. God knows our future and only wants the best for us, many times we get side tracked or we want to do it our way which sometimes causes us to have to go through many trials and tribulations. God loves all His children and He will do whatever it takes to get us to our final goal, Heaven!!

THE LONG JOURNEY

Once there was a man who owned a large plantation, he had two sons and he loved them both very much. He had many servants who worked for him and he treated them all well and they all loved their master and enjoyed working for him because they had heard how other masters had treated their workers some even called them slaves.

As the boys grew up they were different in many ways, they both loved their father, but one of the sons had an inclination to see what the world had in store for him, so he went to his father and asked him if he would give him his inheritance now, he no longer wanted to stay on the farm and continue to work. The father was very sad and tried to talk his son out of leaving, he told him of all the evil out in the world and all the things that could happen to him but the son would not believe anything his father told him. He demanded that if his father really loved him he would give him the money and he would be gone, the boys father finally said ok.

The son now with money in his pockets left the farm and headed for the city, He drank a lot and had many so called friends, he partied every night and slept all day, this went on for awhile and eventually the money ran out. The guy who ran the hotel where he stayed kicked him out, he went to some of his friends houses but they wouldn't let him stay with them either. What was he to do, his money was gone and he had no friends, he had told his father he was going out to conquer the world so he could not go back there. He was going to make a name for himself, he was going to be successful, people every where would recognize him. Now look at me, nothing, what am I supposed to do now. Just happened that a pig farmer saw him sleeping on the street and asked him if he needed a job, at this point he would do anything just to make a buck and get something to eat. As he fed the pigs he would eat some of their food, man where did I go wrong?

Then an idea came to him, I know what I could do. I could go back to my fathers farm and work for him, because everyone who works for him likes it so much, I could tell my father how sorry I was and that I was wrong and made such a mess out of my life, I no longer am worthy to be called his son, just treat me as one of your workers. He practiced what he was going to say over and over on the way back home, he really felt bad about all the mistakes he made, how could his father ever forgive him??

As he topped the hill to the farm he saw his father out in the yard and almost turned around and left because he was so ashamed of all the things he had done, but his father had been looking for him every day, hoping he would someday come home. He began to run to him and as they embraced the son began to say his little speech that he had rehearsed but the father would have none of that, he was still his son and he loved him, no matter what! The father told one of the workers to go and kill the fatted calf, there was going to be a party at our house tonight!!

The other son got wind of what was taking place and boy did he get mad. He asked one of the workers if it was really true that his brother was home and they answered yes and his father was giving him a party. Not only did this make him mad, he became very angry and didn't want any part of it. The father seeing what was happening came to his second son and told him that all that he now possessed was his and that he should be grateful that his brother had returned.

Has this ever happened to you? Work all your life and someone comes along and takes everything that you have worked so hard for? Kind of hard to be happy at a time like this! But you know God is just like the father, he will forgive us, no matter how much of a mess we have made of our lives, He loves us unconditionally, nothing we have ever done can make Him love us less. Don't be like the second son, be happy for your brothers and sisters, they are Gods children too and all the hard work we have done will have it's rewards, God is just and He will take care of all His children!!

THE DUCK

Once upon a time there lived a family in a big city in the east. The mom and dad were raised in the country and they enjoyed talking about all the good times they had growing up. They had two children, Sarah, she was twelve and Sam, he was eight. After school was out and the kids were on summer break mom and dad decided it would be nice if the kids could go and spend the summer with their grandparents who lived on a small farm now because they had sold their large one because it was just too much work for grandpa to take care of, they were getting up in years.

So early one Saturday morning they loaded up and headed for the country, Sarah and Sam were excited because of all the stories they had heard. When they arrived it was just like mom and dad talked about, grandpa had a few cows, some chickens, ducks, even a few pigs and a horse. They enjoyed the weekend and on Sunday afternoon mom and dad headed back to the city leaving their children to live with grandma and grandpa for a couple of months.

Early Monday morning the kids were rolled out of bed at the crack of dawn, they weren't used to getting up this early but they got up and ate and were lined out on the chores that needed done that day, after the chores grandpa was going to take them fishing and show them around the farm. That afternoon grandpa made a slingshot for Sam and showed him how to use it, Sam was excited and he practiced every chance he got, he wasn't very good but he would pretend he was killing mountain lions, bears, he even killed a few make believe deer.

One day as he was coming in from the woods he saw grandma's favorite duck Susie strolling down by the pond, so he picked up a rock and put it in his slingshot and let her rip, poor Susie never saw what was coming, the rock hit her and killed her, Sammie went over and tried to revive her but she was gone. Sam looked up and his sister was standing on the porch and saw the whole thing, he carried Susie around the barn and buried her so no one would find out.

Later after supper grandma asked Sarah to help with the dishes, Sarah said that Sam really wanted to help tonight and she leaned over and told Sam, remember the duck, so Sam said sure grandma, I'd be happy to help you. Next day after their chores grandpa came in with the fishing poles and asked who would like to go fishing, they both jumped up and said me! As they started out the door grandma said she needed help that afternoon with the wash, Sarah said, Sammie will stay and help and whispered in his ear, remember the duck.

This went on for a week and Sammie was getting tired of doing all his and his sisters chores so he came into where grandma was sitting and told her he had some bad news and began telling her about Susie and how he had accidentally had hit her with the slingshot and that he had buried her behind the barn. Grandma just smiled, Sam figured she would be upset and punish him but she just said Sammie, I was standing in the window when you done it and saw the whole thing, I was just waiting to see how long you would let your sister have control over you.

God is just like grandma, He sees everything we do, the good and the bad and He lets us go our way until we find it in our heart to confess to Him, He doesn't get mad at us because He loves us so much and all He wants is for us to be happy, isn't He a GREAT GOD!!!

PSALMS 91: 4

HE WILL COVER YOU WITH HIS
FEATHERS AND UNDER HIS WINGS
YOU CAN HIDE.

PSALMS 121 : 7-8

THE LORD WILL GUARD YOU FROM
ALL EVIL, HE WILL GUARD YOUR
LIFE. THE LORD WILL GUARD YOUR
COMING AND YOUR GOING, BOTH
NOW AND FOREVER.

THE SEED

I heard this story of a C.E.O. who was old and wanted to be replaced,
But he wasn't sure how to pick his successor, for he knew the problems they would face.
So he called a meeting and explained his intentions and gave everyone a seed,
They would take it and let it grow, this would provide the answer he would need.
Young Jim planted his in a large container, watered it everyday,
The other executives did the same, to some it was a game to play.
As months went on they all had stories how their plants were doing fine,
Poor Jim could never get his seed to sprout, and this began to work on his mind.
He talked it over with his wife, I have ruined my chance, I cannot get mine to grow,
Should I go out and buy another plant to replace it, who would ever know?
His wife said "no way, that would be dishonest" he said you're right, I must agree,
But I'll feel so embarrassed when I bring my pot in for everyone to see.
So the time finally came all were asked to bring in, the seed they were given to sow,
As Jim entered in with his empty container, the laughs began to grow.
All the other executives had large hardy plants, Jim felt so ashamed,
The C.E.O. walked in and admired the plants then called out Jims name.
Come stand by me Jim and bring your pot, I have chosen you to succeed,
I told you all when I gave you the seed that it would give me the answer I need.

You see I boiled those seeds before I gave them to you, they were unable
  to sprout
And young Jim standing here is your new C.E.O. because he knows what
  honesty is all about!
How many times in this life are we given a choice, to do right or wrong,
How many times do we compromise, when we know we should be
  strong?
Let this story be an example how we should live our lives, for other people
  to see,
We should never give in just to look good, we should always walk in
  integrity!!

TROUBLE ALONG THE WAY

Earl was a guy who always had a black cloud hanging over his head, it seemed like wherever he went trouble was sure to follow him and today wasn't any different. As Earl made his way along the road a group of robbers attacked him, beat him up and took all his money, but this story isn't about Earl, it is about the people who came down the road after Earls misfortune.

First came a priest, he saw Earl lying there, he could tell he was hurt but he just didn't have the time to deal with it, he was in a hurry, had to be some where and he was running late, so he went to the other side of the road and just kept going.

Next came a Levite, he helps out in the church, kind of a holy man, should have been especially sensitive to Earls predicament, but he too had places to go and people to see, he couldn't take the time to help, so he too just walked on by old Earl. It seems like Earl just couldn't catch a break.

Next came this Samaritan, he was a stranger in this land and everyone kind of looked down on these people, he saw old Earl lying there and had compassion on him. He came over and bound up his wounds, gave him some water and placed him on his own donkey and brought him to the nearest inn, he told the innkeeper to watch over him and give Earl whatever he needed, he gave the innkeeper some money and told him he would be back in a couple of days and if the bill was any more he would pay that too. It seems like Earl had finally caught a break.

Now who would you say was a Christian, the priest surely went to church and had a title. The Levite was a holy man who done all the good deeds at the church, helped in any way he could. What about the Samaritan, he didn't even know Earl, had never met the man, wasn't even the same nationality but he had compassion on Earl, I think that he was the man who showed everyone what it is like to be a Christian. He cared for and had pity on a stranger, took time out of his busy schedule, he even took his own hard earned money and paid for a room, it seems like that is what we all need to do if we really wanted to be a Christian, we need to be more like Christ. He has compassion on all His children and He wants what is best for all of us, shouldn't we try to be imitators of His ways???

THE TRIAL

The scene takes place in a courtroom, could be any courtroom in our modern day society. The person on trial is a middle aged man with long hair and a beard, could be any man in today's society. I have been chosen to plead His case, {poor guy} but I believe in Him and I think He is the person He is representing to be!

For my first witness I call a couple who had just gotten married and was having a reception and what a reception it was, there was a lot of wine flowing and the head master thought it was going to run out which would definitely be a disaster for the young couple so he called the groom over to tell him and Mary just happened to over hear the conversation. She went to her son and told Him about the situation but He seemed unconcerned, but His mother told the servants to follow her sons command, I guess it was then the first miracle took place. He told the servants to go and fill the water crocks with water and take some to the head master, when they did as they were commanded the head master was surprised, usually you would serve the best wine first and then after everyone had drank awhile they would bring out the inferior wine, but this was not the case. They had saved the best wine for last!!

For my second witness I would like to call the dignitary to Galilee, he had a son who was dying and all the doctors in the area had treated him but he grew worse by the hour. One of his servants told him about a healer in town who made people well just by talking to them, what did he have to lose, he told his servant to take him to the healer. As he was talking to my defendant he received word that his son had died, not wanting to bother the healer he turned to leave but another miracle was about to take place for when the dignitary returned home there was his son, alive and well!!

My third witness is a man who was crippled for thirty-eight years, he had laid by this pool in Bethesda because people thought that if you were the first to enter the water when it was stirred you would receive a miracle, this man could never make it because someone would always beat him to the pool so he just laid there until one day my defendant was passing by and He asked the man if he really wanted to walk. Of course I wanted to walk he replied, then my defendant commanded him to get up, take up his pallet and walk, he stood up and walked away!!

For my fourth witness I would like to call this young boy who was in the crowd when my defendant was giving a lecture on the rolling hills of Galilee, there was about five thousand people there and it was getting kind of late. My defendants followers wanted to let the people go because they needed to go and find a place to eat but my defendant told them to feed the crowd. How could we possibly feed this many people, all we have is this young boys lunch, my defendant gave thanks to God and asked Him to bless the fish and bread then told His followers to start passing out the food, everyone had their fill and there was food left over. Another miracle it seems !!

For my fifth witness I would like to call Peter to the stand, he was in the boat the night of the fierce storm and he saw my defendant come to them, walking on the water. Peter was you afraid? Yes, it was the worst storm I had ever seen, water was tossing our boat around like a cork and there He came walking on the water just as if nothing was going on, He told me to come to Him and I got out of the boat and started walking His way when a wave hit me in the face and I began to sink, He reached down and picked me up and He put me back in the boat and told the wind and waves to calm down and they obeyed His command, I couldn't believe my own eyes, I saw it yet I found it hard to believe. I guess you could call this a miracle too!!

As my next witness I would like to call to the stand this man who was born blind, sir how is it you can see now? Well I was sitting by the road one day and I heard this crowd coming down it and asked someone what was going on, he told me the healer was coming down the road, so I began crying out His name and when He came over to me He asked me what I wanted. I told Him that I wanted to see, so He gave me my sight and ever since that day I have been seeing all the wonderful things that God has made and given to His children. I think that too would qualify as a miracle!!

I have one final witness, I have saved the best for last, in fact it is the most awesome thing you will ever hear about. I would like to call Lazarus to the stand. Sir could you tell me in your own words what happened to you? I sure can, I live with my two sisters Martha and Mary, we were very good friends with the defendant, He visited our house on several occasions, everyone loved being around Him. He brought out the best in everyone. Well I became very sick and my sisters thought I was dying so they sent word to our friend and healer and asked Him to come at once, they didn't think I would last through the night. It seems they were right, I died, they waited but our friend never showed up and with the weather being so hot my sisters decided I should be buried, so they laid me in my tomb. It was four days later when He finally showed up and my sisters went to Him crying that I was gone and that they had buried me. I never knew anything, it was like I was in a trance, suddenly I hear His voice calling to me. Lazarus come out, they had rolled the stone from the entrance to my tomb and I heard His voice, immediately I stood up but I couldn't walk because they had wrapped me in my grave cloths. I heard my friend say to the servants, unwrap him and as they did it all came back to me, my sisters told me I had died and they buried me but here I am, the defendant had raised me from the dead I had never heard of such a thing before, but here I am, living proof that God works miracles.

So there you have it, several miracles to different people, all telling you how my defendant has worked miracles in their life, I know He claims to be the Son of God and it may be hard for some people to believe Him but I for one believes that He is who He says He is. You have a whole book written about this Jesus and all the miracles He has performed, read it for yourself, it is called the Bible and you can pick a copy up at any store. See for yourself all the good things He has done then you decide for yourself if He is the Son of God sent down to this Earth to be a Savior to all who believe in Him, you have nothing to lose and an eternity to gain. What verdict will you render??

THE DONKEY STORY

There once was a farmer with a donkey, it fell into a well,
Though it cannot speak for itself, it's story I will tell.
It brayed and brayed to get attention, it needed to help to get out,
The farmer heard it in the well, and he began to shout.
He called his friends and neighbors, they came over right away,
They looked down and saw the donkey, there he'll have to stay.
Each found a shovel and started throwing, dirt upon his back,
The donkey it just brayed and brayed, but soon it got on track.
He would just shake the dirt away, then he would step up,
The farmers kept on shoveling, like filling up a cup!
Soon the donkey was at the top, he just walked away,
The farmers stood and scratched their heads, but I have more say.
We are like the donkey, sometimes we get down,
The devil tries to cover us, and take away our crown.
But we must learn to shake it off, experience lifts us to the top,
And if we learn from trials and errors, the devil soon will stop!
We can take all the bad, and turn it into good,
God is with us helping out, like He said He would.
So the next time the devil comes at you, and tries to harden you like a
    stone,
Just shake it off and say to him, I am not alone.
Cause Jesus lives inside me, He shows me the way,
And I am going to follow Him, each and every day!!

THE FIRST CHRISTMAS

Long ago, just after God the Father had created the Universe, He had a plan to create beings to live in heaven. He created the angels, there are several different kinds of angels, some just serve God, others are like soldiers who protect heaven, then there are those who are called messengers and finally those who are called to guard all God's children, just like you and me. Things had been going just fine in heaven for many years and God loved all that He had created because God is Love. One day the mightiest of all angels, his name was Lucifer, called many of the angels together and tried to take over heaven, he was the strongest and brightest angel that was ever created and he thought he was just as powerful as God, the One who had created him in the first place. He felt like he could rule heaven better than God, so he got a lot of the angels and told them lies and he said that heaven under his rule would be better than it is now with God in charge. He told them all the things he could make better and many believed his lies and followed him.

There was a great battle in Heaven between Lucifer and all the bad angels who tried to take over, and Michael who was captain of all the good angels. God knew what their plan was and He had already informed Michael about the battle and the plan was to defeat the bad angels and send them to this place called Earth. There they would spend eternity and would not have all the beauties and wonders that Heaven had in store for all those who believed in God and followed His commands. The battle took place and Michael defeated Lucifer and now he was sent to Earth, at this time Earth was just a black planet, no water, or trees, or animals, Lucifer didn't like it here because he missed all the wonderful things that he had grown accustomed to in Heaven but he had no choice, that was to be his punishment.

Things got back to normal in Heaven after a short time but now Heaven seemed empty because so many of the angels were now gone, they had decided to follow Lucifer and their punishment was the same as his, they lived on this cold black planet too!

God decided He would fill Heaven back up, so He came up with this plan, He was going to create human beings, just like you and me, since God did not want the same thing to happen again He was going to create everyone and give them a will, that way, each person could decide weather they wanted to serve God and live in Heaven or be like Lucifer. He would place a part of Himself in each person, that way they would live forever, He would give them a human body and a spirit, they would be sent to Earth to live for a period of time and when they had made up their mind where they would like to live forever God would honor their request.

Since Earth was a very black and miserable place He decided to make Earth more beautiful. He created stars and the sun, oceans and dry lands, He even created animals, birds and fish. He tried to make it like Heaven in many ways. He created mountains, hills and valleys, He placed streams of water and rivers that ran throughout the land, He created fruit trees for food and all kinds of wonderful plants and flowers. All of His creation was wonderful, so now He created His first human beings, they were male and female and He called them Adam and Eve. He placed them in this wonderful garden and told them they could enjoy everything that was around them except for one tree that grew in the middle of the garden, He told them if they ate the fruit of that tree that they would surely die. God knew what our decision would be before we were ever placed there and He had another plan already in place.

So Adam and Eve enjoyed the garden, they didn't have to work or sweat, everything they needed was provided for them, they were very happy for a short while. Then along came Lucifer, he saw what Gods plan was and he was going to persuade the human beings to follow him and not God, remember, God gives every single person a will to choose, it is up to each of us to choose who we will follow. So one day as Eve was walking in the garden Lucifer came up to Eve and told her how if she would just eat of the fruit that was in the center of the garden she would become as wise as God. At first she didn't want to do it but Lucifer was very persistent, finally Eve gave in and took a bite, upon seeing it was good she called Adam over to enjoy the fruit too, after Adam had tried it they realized they were naked and they made some cloths out of the leaves from the trees. That evening when God entered the garden to talk with them they hid, God called out their names and they came out, He asked why they were hiding and they answered they were naked and God knew that they had eaten from the forbidden tree.

God now must drive them from the garden and He got angry with Lucifer, He would now be known as Satan or the devil, He told Adam and Eve that from now on they would have to work for their food and cloths. They would have children and reproduce offspring, that way in years to come there would be enough people to fill all the kingdom of Heaven. So they left the garden and found a cave to live in, to eat they would gather the nuts and fruits form the trees, God showed them how to plant seeds for other things to grow, it was hard but they now worked for all their food, He gave them animals to kill for food and they made cloths out of their skins. God showed them many things and helped them, he told them that they would grow old and eventually they would die, but only their human body would die, their spirit would live on forever and that He had another plan that later He would put into action. God was going to take on the human form and be born as a baby, He would suffer for all the sins of man and whoever believed in this God made man would again return to the beauty and joy of Heaven.

Adam and Eve had children, just like we still do today. They were married and had other children and the Earth began to be filled with people, but remember Satan, he still wanted everyone to follow him, so he tried every trick he knew to try and convince the people to follow him. He had most of the people following him and God saw how evil and corrupt the world had become, so God called the only good man left on Earth and told him that He was going to flood the Earth, that he needed to build a huge ship and that he [Noah] and his family must get aboard the ark and take two of every kind of animal with them. After the flood and all the people had perished God sent word to Noah to come out of the ark and they would have to start all over again. So Noah and his three sons and their wives began having more children and people once more filled the Earth. God placed a rainbow in the sky as His promise that no more would He flood the Earth with water.

As more people began to inhabit the Earth cities were formed, then countries. Towns grew and the people reverted back to their old ways, it seemed like Satan had an effect on many people and God was once again being forgotten, except for one tribe of people, the Jews, they continued to worship God as their one true God. The other people had many things that they worshipped and called them gods, but very soon God was going to send His only Son upon the Earth, He would be called Jesus, He would be the Savior of all mankind.

God called the angel Gabriel to His throne and told him it was time for Jesus to make His appearance upon the Earth, God sent Gabriel down to the small town of Nazareth, there he would find a virgin by the name of Mary she would become the mother of Jesus. So Gabriel entered Mary's home and said, "Peace to you, do not fear, for you have found favor with God and you are to bear His Son, you will call Him Jesus." at first Mary was afraid but she answered, "Be it done as you say" and the power of the Holy Spirit overshadowed her and she became with child, for nothing is impossible with God.

Mary was supposed to get married to a young carpenter named Joseph and when the time had come to wed, Joseph found out that she was with child. This upset Joseph very much but that night as he slept an angel appeared to Joseph in a dream and told him what had happened so that when he awakened he went ahead and took Mary to be his wife. After they were married Mary went to visit her cousin Elizabeth because she was going to have a baby also, his name was going to be John, later he would go out and tell the people about Jesus who had come to save the world.

Just like now, there was going to be a census taken, that is they have to count all the people, Mary and Joseph had to go to a small town of Bethlehem because that is where Josephs family was from there they would register, by this time Mary was getting very close to the time that she was going to have her baby. As they came to Bethlehem they searched every where but there was no room at any of the inn's, finally an inn keeper said they could stay in the stable with the cows and sheep because Mary's time had come to deliver her baby.

Joseph made Mary a bed in the straw and took the feed trough and made a crib for the baby Jesus. There Jesus was born, as the cows, sheep and donkeys looked on, Jesus made His appearance into this world. In a field the shepherds lay watching their sheep and all of a sudden the whole sky burst forth with angels singing praise to the baby Jesus. The shepherds didn't know what was going on they became frightened, but one of the angels told them that a Savior had been born in a stable and his name was Jesus, if they would go there they could see Him, so it was, the poor shepherds were the first to see the newborn child. Instead of being born in a palace with rich people all around Jesus had chosen to be born in a stable with animals looking on. Hands that created the universe now were so tiny that they couldn't even pick up a bottle, Jesus who was a King lying in a trough that the animals ate out of, He could have been born anywhere but He chose the lowliest place on Earth. I sometimes wonder why He did that, but then I think of all the love He has for us, it's not about the gold and silver, it's not about being well known or the richest, it is all about His love for us, He came that we may live in Heaven forever. The wise men who saw the star in the East followed it till it came to rest over the house where Jesus now lived. They brought with them, gold, frankincense and myrrh. Gold because Jesus was royalty, frankincense because Jesus was the true high priest who would offer up His body to be sacrificed for our sins and myrrh because that is what people back then used to anoint a body before they laid it in the tomb. He gave us the greatest Christmas present that anyone could ever give, He gave His life for us, and anyone who believes in Him shall not perish, but will have life for all Eternity. That was Gods greatest plan and Satan may try to deceive the people, but in the end it is Jesus who triumphs over the world.

It all began thousands of years ago and no one knows how long it will continue but one thing is for sure. God is love and He wants the best for all His children, He will never leave you alone, He will answer when you call on Him, you can never fall so far that He cannot reach down and pick you up, no matter what kind of a mess you get into. He gave us a free will and we can always choose what we want to do, with Jesus in our hearts our choice will always be the right one. So have a Merry Christmas and may you never ever forget the real reason why there is a Christmas, Jesus came upon this Earth to save all His children because He doesn't want anyone to miss out on Heaven, that is why we were born in the first place, to take our place with God and share in all the wonderful things that He has in store for us when we finally make it home. Thank You Jesus!!!

THE VINEYARD

The reign of God is like the owner of this vineyard, he needed workers to work his fields, so he went out early that morning and he found men standing around. He asked them if they would like to work in his vineyard and they said yes, so he agreed to pay them a fair days wage, they agreed and went forth to his vineyard.

About mid morning he went again and there were men standing around, so he asked them if they would like to work in his vineyard, they answered yes, he told them he would pay them and they left to go to work in his fields.

At noon he went back out and once again he found men just standing around, they too agreed to go to work at his vineyards. At mid-afternoon he went out and once again he found men standing there not doing anything, he asked them if they would like to work and they said yes, so he told them to go to his vineyard they would be told what to do.

When evening finally came the owner told the servants to pay the workers but to begin with those who arrived last. When the workers who were hired first saw how much they were getting, they at once thought that they were going to receive more since they had labored all day, but when they received the same thing they got angry at the owner. They asked why they had received the same amount as the men who had only worked a few hours. The owner asked them if they were jealous of his generosity, didn't he pay them what they had agreed on that morning, they said yes but it wasn't right because they had worked all day out in the hot sun and these last workers had worked only a few hours.

Isn't it like that today, some people have served God since they were a small child, others were converted in their youth, some were adults when they asked Jesus to be there Savior, then there are those who wait till their death bed to receive Jesus. Should we be angry at God for saving anyone, isn't it through His goodness and grace that we are saved, the way I look at it. We have just enjoyed all His goodness and grace all of our lives and I am thankful that He extends His grace to all who will receive it. We should be happy for all our brothers and sisters who accept Christ because we are all Gods children and one day we will all be united in Heaven to live forever in the glory of our God!!!

BE READY AT ALL TIMES

The kingdom of God could be compared to the ten virgins. They were told that the bride and groom were coming that evening, so they took their lamps and went and stayed by the road that led to the hall. Five of them were wise and the other five were not thinking to clearly.

The wise brought extra oil, but the foolish figured they had enough to last the night. They waited for a very long time and it was getting kind of late, the foolish virgins asked those who had brought extra oil for some of theirs, but they answered back, we only have enough for our lamps, if you need some you still have time to go and buy it. So the five foolish left to go to Wal-mart to buy some more oil, while they were gone the bride and groom came by and they all went to the hall. After they had entered, the doors were locked behind them. Later the five who had left came to the door and knocked and wanted to be let in, the groom came over and looked out at them but he would not open the door because he did not know them..

It may also be like the wedding feast that this king was going to give. He invited many people to his feast, so when the time came, he sent out his servants who told the people that the feast was ready. Many had excuses, some had bought a house they couldn't come, others had bought some cows, they couldn't come, some just didn't feel like coming, so when evening came the hall was just half filled. Now the king sent out his servants to the shopping centers and the road houses and the movie theaters and told them to bring everyone they saw. After this the hall was full and the king was very happy. As he made his way around the guests he saw that some did not have on the proper garments and when he asked them why, they couldn't answer, so he told the servants to throw them out since they were not dressed for the occasion.

Kind of like us, we never know when God is going to call us home, we may be out shopping or having a good time, we may not be ready to go yet but that doesn't matter. When our time has come to an end we are going to go to the feast and we had better have on the proper clothes, we don't want to be cast out of Heaven, if you don't know what clothes I'm talking about, it is the salvation of Jesus. He is the only One who is worthy and we are made worthy through His righteousness. So be ready at all times, you will never know the time or place!!!

THE WORD

A farmer went out one time to sow some seed. Some of the seed landed on a path where birds came along and ate it up. Some of it landed in the rocks and since there was no soil it sprouted, but soon it withered away. Some landed in the briars and thorns, it started to grow but then it got choked out. Some of it landed on good soil, this seed grew and it produced much grain.

Jesus asked His apostles if they understood this story and they all answered no, so He told it to them in a different way. The farmer is God and the seed is the word of God. The word lands in the heart of some people but their heart are so hard that they can't believe a word of it. Then there are those who hear the word, they start to believe for awhile but not having any roots they soon forget all about it. There is also ones who hear the word and for awhile they are very happy, they understand it and want to follow Gods' ways, but along comes Satan and convinces them that this word is all wrong, it doesn't mean what they think it means. Then there are those who hear the word and believe it is from God, they read it every day and they tell all their friends and neighbors about it and many are convinced that God is real and He wants the very best for all His children.

What type of soil do you have in your heart, is it so hard that you can't believe anything that pertains to God, maybe you want to believe but others tell you it is all a bunch of nonsense, God isn't real and there is no such place as Heaven. Maybe when you were a child someone told you about God but you can't see Him, so He must not be real. Could it be you believe in God but every day you grow a little further away, you would like to trust in Him but everyone around you tries to convince you He is not to be trusted, He will disappoint you when you need Him the most. Maybe you are the type who believes God is real, you can feel Him in your heart, you can feel His love, you know He is watching over you. You want to tell everyone you meet about how good He is and all the good things He has in store for those who believe. That is the person I am, I couldn't even imagine a life without Him, I feel His presence, I feel His love and I truly wish everyone could feel the way I do, but I know they don't. Maybe someday when He returns to take His children home all will be convinced of His love, I just hope it won't be too late for some people!!!!

WITHOUT GOD WE CANNOT-WITHOUT US GOD WILLNOT

Without God in our lives we are helpless,
Without Jesus in our lives we are hopeless.
When things are darkest in our lives, God lights the way,
When things seem impossible to us, God keeps us from going astray.
When we have fallen or don't know which way to turn, He leads us,
When we have sinned He doesn't forsake, for He is just.
God shows us mercy, though we don't deserve it,
He gives salvation, but we must want it.
For even though He is Almighty and all Powerful, He is still God,
He gives us wills to choose, though sometimes I find that quite odd.
He could have made us to love Him, but this is not His way,
We must choose to follow Him, each and every day !
He will not say, "Do My Will", but lets us decide,
We can choose right or wrong, how do you feel inside?
God would like for everyone, to always do what's right,
For the battle between good and evil, is a constant fight.
But God will not do it all, the decision is ours to make,
He won't force His will on us, so do not hesitate.
Give your will to our heavenly Father, be all you can be,
Then you'll share in His joy and love, for all eternity !!

1 JOHN 2: 1-2

I AM WRITING THIS TO KEEP YOU FROM SIN, BUT IF ANYONE SHOULD SIN, WE HAVE, IN THE PRESENCE OF THE FATHER, JESUS CHRIST, AN INTERSESSOR WHO IS JUST. HE IS AN OFFERING FOR OUR SINS, AND NOT ONLY AN OFFERING FOR OUR SINS, BUT FOR THE WHOLE WORLD.

YOU ARE MY SUNSHINE

I heard a story about this young boy, we'll call him Timmy, he found out his mother was going to have a baby sister. She took Timmy to the doctor when she went for her checkups and he could see the baby move in his mommies tummy. Timmy was only five and his mother explained everything that was going on, how his little sister was growing and when the time came she would be born just like he was. Everyday Timmy would lay on his mothers lap and sing, You are my sunshine, to his little sister and talk to her and feel her move around in his mommies tummy, he was always asking questions and his mom would answer them as best as she could.

This went on for months and the time finally arrived for his sister to be born, so they all rushed to the hospital. There was some complications and the baby was finally born but there was a problem, so the doctor had to take his sister to the pre natal intensive care unit and he told Timmy's parents that he didn't think the baby would make it. They were so worried and didn't want to tell Timmy about her condition but he kept asking when he was going to get to see her. Finally realizing this may be the only chance for Timmy to see her she snuck him in the intensive care unit to see her. When he saw her and his mother told him how sick she was Timmy began singing, You are my sunshine, to his baby sister, the head nurse heard him and asked how this child had gotten into the intensive care area, young children are not allowed in there and they would have to remove him at once.

That is when the miracle took place, the babies heart rate began to drop and she was more relaxed, the nurse upon seeing the babies response told Timmy to keep on singing to her, as he did her rate began to drop to normal and the baby was now resting comfortably. After a few days it looked like everything was now normal and Timmy's family got to take his little sister home.

God works miracles everyday, it may not be earth shaking but to Timmy and his family this was the best miracle he could ever have gotten. Sometimes God speaks to us through small every day happenings, if our hearts are open to God's ways we can see them. Are you open to God's voice, many times He speaks to us through His written word, sometimes it is only a still small voice of a child, are you listening to see if He is speaking to you????

HOLIDAYS, SEASONS FOR JOYS OR TROUBLES

Once upon a time there was a young couple, they had only been married for a short time, but it seemed every time a holiday approached there was a lot of tension that existed between them.

They both came from rather large families and they both wanted to spend time with their own families, but it seemed like there just wasn't enough hours in the day.

Then along came their first baby, now it was even harder than before. Both families wanted more time with their grandchild, the families didn't like being left out on holidays, it seemed like some one needed to give a little, life was becoming such a strain on the young couple. How could they please each family and still have time to work on their relationship, holidays started to become a real hassle, they couldn't please every one no matter what they did. The wife felt like they should spend time with her family because after all, her and her mother-in-law could never see eye to eye on certain things. The husband wanted to spend time with his family because they were older in age and you never know how much longer they would be around, so the strain now was becoming a burden and holidays now were something they both began to dread. The tension began to grow in their relationship, was there some solution to their growing problem or would they just have to try and do the best they could with the situation that they were in.

They came up with a solution for their problem, on holidays they would spend time with one side one day and the next day they would spend time with the other side. Seemed like a good plan but what day would they go to the wife's family and what day would they go to the husbands family. Another problem, it seems like they couldn't get together on that either, now tension began to grow even worse.

The wife felt like it wasn't all her problem and she decided to just go to her family, her husband could come along if he wanted to or do what ever he wanted. The husband didn't think that was right, so he just went to his side of the family, only one problem now, where was the baby going? If she took her with her was it fair to the husbands mom and dad? If she let her child go with her dad was it fair to her mom and dad? The problem just continued to get worse and the tension began to show in their marriage. Now the problem just wasn't the holidays any more, it was an everyday thing. They both began to feel like the love they once had just wasn't there anymore. What had happened to the loving relationship they once enjoyed, how could they ever get back to the place they once were? Everything was so easy when they were just dating, these problems never arose, but now with the baby and their life together it seemed like there was just no solution to there problem. There were several options they could choose, but which one was the best.

Are you in a situation like this now, has your life become stressed out because of the holidays, do you need a solution for what you need to do? It would be easy if there was one simple answer, but there isn't. Every couple has to deal with that on there own, on a one to one basis. I can tell you from experience, it doesn't get any better by not dealing with it. Someone is going to be hurt, you just have to way the solution out and talk it over. Put yourself on both sides of the fence, look at it from both sides of the family, talk it out. Don't let a beautiful relationship be ruined by your family, after all, now you are a family too!

I wish I could say, do it this way and everything will be fine but I can't, it has to be a solution that you both have to reach. Don't let the holidays become such a drag that you hate to even see one come around, after all, you have your whole life ahead of you, enjoy it together!!!

TOSSED AT SEA

There is a story I once heard about this business man who came to town late one night, he flagged down a taxi and told the driver to take him to his hotel, he gave him the address and asked him if he knew where it was, the cabbie said yes, I have been there several times. The man felt confident so he laid back in his seat and decided to take a nap on the way. After about fifteen minutes he woke up and tapped the cabbie on the shoulder, immediately he swerved from side to side before finally coming to a complete stop on the side of the road. He turned around and apologized to the man for nearly wrecking the cab, he told him this was his first day as a cabbie, he had been driving a hearse for ten years.

What fears do you have? Are you afraid that you will die from some accident or sickness, maybe your afraid you will run out of money before you run out of time. There are so many things to worry about in this world but I have good news for you. God has given us several commands in the Bible to fear not, why is it we believe some of the things in the Bible, but when it comes to fear we can't stop worrying. Hasn't God showed us that He is well cable of handling any problems that might arise?

In Mark chapter 4 verses 35-41 he tells us the story about Jesus being asleep in the back of the boat and this giant storm comes up and is tossing the boat around like a cork. The apostles were afraid that any minute they were going to go down to the bottom of the lake. Finally they awakened Jesus and asked Him if He cared that they were about to be drowned, Jesus stood up and calmed the seas and the wind and asked why they were so afraid, where is your faith? Any one of the apostles could have calmed the seas and the wind if they had only done it in Jesus' name. We have great power in Jesus' name, but too often we forget about it, He tells us that He has sent the Spirit to live inside of us, so we have the same power as Jesus, only thing is, we don't have the faith. Sometimes when you are faced with a problem that seems too big for you to handle and you become afraid try talking to your problem in the name of Jesus, see what happens.

You'll never know if you never try. Jesus tells us to "Fear Not, for I am with you." And if He be for us, who could be against us???

GALATIONS 4: 7

AND YOU NEVER AGAIN HAVE TO WONDER WHO YOUR FATHER IS, YOU'VE BEEN ADOPTED BY GOD AND ARE THEREFORE AN "HEIR OF GOD THROUGH CHRIST JESUS."

ROMANS 5: 1

THROUGH CHRIST'S SACRIFICE, OUR PAST IS PARDONED AND OUR FUTURE SECURE. And "SINCE WE HAVE BEEN MADE RIGHT WITH GOD BY OUR FAITH, WE HAVE PEACE WITH GOD."

ONE DAY

One day in Gods court is like a thousand elsewhere,
The pain and sorrow you feel on Earth, is more than you can bear.
I wish I could return for just an hour, to show you Heaven is real,
I wish I could take your hurt and pain, and show you the love I feel.
On Earth there are so many trials and challenges you must face,
But in Heaven God is Love, and we are filled by His Grace.
Time flew by so fast on Earth, days became months, then years,
We never knew what tomorrow held, our lives were filled with fears.
Forgiveness was tough, our feelings got hurt, life could be so hard,
But up in Heaven love abounds, it is truly our reward.
If I could tell you just one thing to help your circumstance,
It would be this, "Give everyday a chance!".
Look around at other people, how can I help them out,
After all, life is short, and this is what love is all about.
You never know when your life is done, when you'll be called to rest,
But you'll need not worry or have a fear, when you have done your best.
Love and care like there is no tomorrow, don't be afraid to begin,
And if God blesses you with another day, love and care again!
And when you draw your final breath and your life on Earth is through,
That is when your life will finally begin, and I'll be here for you!!

THE SHOES

There was this lady walking down this busy sidewalk when she happened to notice this small boy standing at the window looking in, she noticed he was barefoot and the weather was starting to get cold. She walked over and asked him his name and he looked up and said "My name is Toby." She said, well Toby what are you doing on this busy sidewalk all alone? He told her he was asking God for a pair of shoes. She took him by the hand and they walked into the store, she asked the sales clerk if she had a pan of water and took Toby to the back and washed his feet. Then she asked the clerk to bring a bundle of socks and a pair of shoes for Toby. When she had washed his feet she put the socks on and tied the rest in a bundle to take with him, then she placed the new shoes on his feet. She noticed young Toby was crying so she asked what was wrong. He looked up at her and asked "Are you Gods' wife?"

How many times do we see someone in distress and we just walk on by, we don't have the time, we don't have the money, maybe even if we did we just don't really care. How much better this world would be if we all took the time to help just one person a week.

In the gospels there are many stories about how Jesus went around helping everyone He met, He gives us the Golden Rule to live by. Treat others the way you would have them treat you. Have you ever stopped and thought about those words, how do you want to be treated? It reminds me of a story in the Bible.

Jesus was in this room with His apostles and they were going to celebrate the feast of the Passover and He got a pan of water and a towel and went around to everyone and washed their feet. Back then this was the servants job, he had to wash all the guests feet before a meal. At first they didn't want to let Him do it, but He told them it had to be done as an example to all, if He could wash their feet, then they in turn should wash the feet of those around them. Jesus used this act to show them that no one is any better than anyone else, we should help each other. It could be with our time, our money or maybe with our abilities. We all have different skills, I like to write, if I can help someone with a story or a word then I ask God to help these words open up hearts that have been closed and I give Him all the glory!!

THE GARDEN

The garden was a place that everyone longs to live, it had all kinds of fruit trees, plenty to eat and you never had to labor, everything just came to you and you had no problems. Seems like a really nice place, how do you get there you ask? It seems like our ancestors started out there but they got wrapped up in the one thing they couldn't have compared to all the things that they had at their fingertips. Doesn't that seem odd, kind of like today, we can have everything we need to survive but there is always something better over the next hill or around the next turn. It seems like the grass is always greener on the other side! We just can't be satisfied with the life we have, we are always looking for that place over the rainbow, but the more we search, the farther away it gets, life can be such a hassle at times.

I have read stories about this garden, it seems like we are always given a choice, we have to choose from what is good for us and what we think might be good for us and too many times we choose the wrong things. Do you ever wonder if you would have taken a bite of the apple from the forbidden tree? You know we still have to make choices everyday, it may not have the same consequences but it surely effects where we will spend Eternity! Where do you want to go when you draw your final breath? Many people never even think about it, some just don't really care and others don't know what to do about it. What class are you in, or do you know where you are headed? I know where I am going and I would like to take as many people with me as I can, that is why I try to do my best even though sometimes my best isn't good enough. That is why we have a Savior called Jesus, He is God made Man, He came down on this Earth to get a taste of the trials we go through, He can relate to what we go through on this journey we call life. He has been tempted just like we are, only one thing different, he never gave in to the temptations!

No tears, no sorrows, no more being tempted to do the wrong thing, sounds like a perfect garden to me, won't you join me on my journey? It is quite simple, just ask Jesus to come into your life, tell Him you are sorry for all the wrongs you have ever done, believe that He is the Son of God and that He is coming back to take you home. This won't make all your troubles go away, but it will bring you a lot of peace just knowing where you will spend Eternity! See you in the Garden!!!

THE END

When the end finally comes, and you draw your last breath,
Who's going to cry, at the news of your death?
Did you spend all your time, at work or at play,
Or did you take time, to stop and pray?
Was God number one, or two, or three,
Did He live in your heart, for others to see.
It's easy to get sidetracked, there's so much to do,
Is that what the people, are going to say about you?
Oh how he partied, the fun never stopped,
He laughed and he drank, till the day he dropped.
Or maybe you worked, long hours on the job,
Never seeing the tears, or hearing the sob.
Your family was there, but you never took the time,
You were important, you had a ladder to climb.
I'll go see Jason play ball, or watch Susie dance,
But what if something happens, and you never get the chance?
You live only once, the time flies by,
You don't know the day, or time you will die.
Stop, look, and listen, to your heart today,
It has something important, it's trying to say!
Only you can open it, and let Jesus inside,
Maybe it's time, you swallowed your pride.
Confess all your sins, we all have a few,
Is that what the Spirit, is asking you do?
Don't wait another day, it may never come,
Don't put it off, till tomorrow like some.
You may say, "I'm still young, I have places to go and see,
I'll get around to it, you can count on me!

I'm a pretty good guy, I do what is right,
Don't ask me, to accept Jesus tonight.
I'll live my life, and when the time gets near,
I'll get right with God, I have nothing to fear".
But what if tonight, when you lay down to sleep,
Your life is required, and no one hears a peep.
You draw your last breath, your time has run out,
Will those who come to mourn you, have any doubt?
So live each day, like there's no tomorrow,
So those who love you, don't go through this sorrow.
With Jesus in your heart, when you go to rest,
Everyone will know, you gave it your best!!

TOBIT 13, 16-18

THE GATES OF JERUSALEM SHALL BE BUILT WITH SAPPIRE AND EMERALD AND ALL YOUR WALLS WITH PRECIOUS STONES. THE TOWERS OF JERUSALEM SHALL BE BUILT WITH GOLD. THE STREETS OF JERUSALEM SHALL BE PAVED WITH RUBIES AND STONES OF OPHIR. THE GATES OF JERUSALEM SHALL SING HYMNS OF GLADNESS AND ALL HER HOUSES SHALL CRY OUT, "ALLELUIA, BLESSED BE GOD WHO HAS RAISED YOU UP!"

I COULD HAVE

[IN MEMORY OF JASON CALLAHAN]

I could have told him about Jesus' love, maybe next time.
I could have told him about Jesus' grace, maybe tomorrow.
I could have told him about how Jesus came to save, maybe later.
I could have told him about Heaven and Eternity, I'll get around to it.
I could have told him Jesus was the Way, the Truth and the Life, maybe
   next week.
I could have been sure where he would spend Eternity, but now it's too
   late!
You see, none of us is guaranteed another tomorrow, today may be all we
   have left.
I could have made a difference, but I put it off!
My only consolation is a passage in Mathew 18:14,
"Even so, it is not the will of your Father who is in Heaven, that even one
   of these should perish !"
I could have, I should have, but now I'll never get the chance!!

THE STORY OF ADAM AND EVE

On the sixth day God created man, He formed him out of the earth and breathed in him the breath of life, this is the Spirit, it will live on for all eternity. As Adam and God walked through the garden he began giving names to all the animals God had created, when they had completed this Adam noticed that all the animals had a mate, but he had no one, so he asked God where was his mate. God told Adam that He would create someone who would do all his chores, take care of all his needs, cook his meals and do his laundry, be at his beckon call at all times. Adam was very much impressed and he asked God just exactly how much this was going to cost? God told Adam that this would cost him an arm and a leg, Adam thought about it for awhile and then asked God what he could get for just a rib and the rest is just history!

Really, God cast a spell over Adam and took out one of his ribs and formed another being similar to Adam, God breathed His Spirit into that being and when Adam woke up from his sleep God presented Eve to Adam. Adam said, at last, she is bone of my bone, flesh of my flesh, this one I will call 'women'. That is why a man shall leave his father and mother and cling to his wife, and the two of them shall become one body. Adam and Eve was given a free will, that meant they could make there own choice of what they wanted to do, they didn't know, but later that free will would get them into a lot of trouble.

God talked with them every day, He told them of all the things in the Garden, He explained life to them and showed them many things, He only had one rule. DO NOT EAT OF THE FRUIT FROM THE TREE IN THE MIDDLE OF THE GARDEN, IF YOU EAT IT YOU WILL SURELY DIE!! That should have been easy because they had many other trees that had fruit on them and they could eat from any of those. That gift of the free will would cause everyone who would ever be born a lot of headaches. We say if that was us, we wouldn't have eaten from that tree, but how many times do we disobey Gods laws even today. God gave us the free will to choose because He didn't want anyone in Heaven there unless they wanted to be there, so He made it easy, we can choose where we want to spend Eternity. He tells us in many ways and all throughout the Bible, CHOOSE LIFE! But still, many people don't listen to His word, what choices are you making. Heaven, or Hell, the choice is yours!!!

ALADDIN

Remember the story of Aladdin, he was walking along the shore and he found this lamp in the sand. As he wiped it off a genie came out and told him that his wish was his command. Anything that young Aladdin wanted was at his fingertips, he only had to wish for it and the genie would make it happen. Many of us look at God in this fashion, we think He is our genie and when we ask for something He is supposed to make it happen. We try to keep Him in a bottle or a lamp and we only want to let Him out when we need something that we can't do on our own. If we are going through a hard time or we have a challenge that is just too difficult for us to handle it is time for us to get on our knees and pray, we call out His name, we make promises, we will do anything He wants, if only He will help us out. Have you been there, do you know what I am talking about, is this how you see the Creator of the Universe? Many people do and even I do it at times. I was brought up as a Catholic and went to a Catholic school where religion was taught to us just like reading, writing and arithmetic. We read all the stories in the Bible and were taught how good God was and how He only wants what is best for us. We learned of all the miracles that His Son Jesus performed when He came down to Earth to die for our sins so that one day we may be up in Heaven and enjoy all the good things God has prepared for us. We learned that God is Love and that He loves us in spite of anything we do, we can never fall too far, or get into so much trouble that He can't get us out. We were taught that nothing is impossible with God and you know what, I still believe all that I was taught as a young child. There is NOTHING that God cannot do if we will only believe in Him. He doesn't want to be some genie in a bottle though, He wants to be a part of our lives every moment, every decision we make He wants to be a part of it because He tells us that if He be for us, who can be against us. We have to include Him in everything we do, we have to believe that everywhere we go, He is there with us, just like in Psalm 23. Though I walk through the valley of death, He will be with us, His rod and staff to guide us and protect us. What an awesome and Mighty God we serve, do you know Him? Would you like to know more about Him? Pick up a copy of His Word, it is called the Bible, see for yourself all the wonderful things He has done and how much He loves us and all the good things He has in store for us!!!

TOBIAH

Tobiah was a young man, son of Tobit, he set out on a journey to his relatives to find Sarah, the girl he was going to marry. The angel Raphael was with him, but he didn't know that he was an angel, he thought he was just a friend that his father had hired to protect him on his journey. That night as it got dark they fished for food for them to eat, Raphael told Tobiah to clean the fish, but to save the heart, the gall and the liver, he would need it later to cure his fathers eyes and to drive away the evil spirits that possessed Sarah. When they got to Raguel's house they entered and met them for the first time, Raguel did not know that Tobiah was Tobit's son, but he could see that he looked like him. After they had talked for awhile he asked for Sarah's hand in marriage and Raguel agreed and they had a feast to celebrate the occasion. Raguel told Tobiah that she had been married seven times before, but on each occasion as the groom entered her room they had died of some unknown cause, no one knew that she was to be Tobiahs wife from the beginning of time, so they were married.

As the feast was coming to an end that night Raphael told Tobiah to take the fish liver and heart into Sarah's room with him and place it on the bed of coals and the smoke from them would drive the evil spirit away, so he did as he was told and the spirit departed. Before they went to bed they prayed to the Lord to have mercy on them and protect them. The next day Sarah's parents were surprised to see that Tobiah had made it through the night, then they began the wedding celebration which lasted for fourteen days.

Tobiah, Raphael and Sarah needed to get back to Tobit's house because he was worried that something bad had happened to his son, but when they got there he saw that everything was ok and that he had taken Sarah for his wife. They all rejoiced and Tobiah took the fish gall and rubbed it in his fathers eyes and they were healed. Later they tried to pay Raphael for all that he had done, but he refused and told them that he was an angel sent from God and they all gave praise to God and lived a happy and peace filled life.

God has all our lives planned out if we would just follow His ways, but too many times we want to do what we think is best for us. Wouldn't it be nice if we knew how it all would end!!!

ESTHER

Ester was a young Jewish maiden, she had an uncle Mordecai who lived in the court to king Xerxes who ruled Persia. She never thought that one day she would be a queen, but God had other plans for her. Mordecai herd two guards plotting to kill the king and he went and told the king about it, upon investigation they confessed and were put to death. This brought Mordecai much favor with the king and he was placed in the kings court.

One day the king gave a banquet and invited everyone to come and partake, but queen Vashti would not come, this angered the king and he called together his court and asked them what he should do. They told the king that if he didn't punish her somehow that all the wives in his nation would rebel against their husbands and great trouble would come over his kingdom. He agreed, so he took her crown away from her, she was no longer queen of Persia. After awhile he felt he needed a queen, so he sent out a decree for maidens to come to his court to be judged who would become the next queen. Mordecai had a niece who was very beautiful and he had her come to be judged, she was a Jew, Jews were hated at that time, so he told Ester not to tell anyone she was a Jew.

For months the young maidens were groomed to come before the king, then when it finally came Ester's turn she entered his court and he immediately fell in love with her, she became queen of all Persia.

The plot to kill king Xerxes was still being planned by some of the officials in his court. One night Mordecai heard of another plan and he went to Ester and told her about it. She told the king and the plot was uncovered and these too were hanged. Ester had great favor with the king and she was by far the most favored of all the kings wives.

After all these plots against his life king Xerxes decided he would appoint Haman over his court, he would answer only to the king, now all the people would have to bow down to him when he entered the court.

Mordecai would not bow down to Haman because he only bowed to the most High God and this made Haman very angry, so he came up with a plan, he would destroy all the Jews throughout the land. Haman came before the king and told him that there was a certain race of people in his land that would not honor his request and that they needed to be wiped out before they came up with a plot to overthrow him. The king fearing this action sent out a decree that all the Jews would be exterminated on the thirteenth day of the twelfth month, now Mordecai saw this decree and knew he must act fast if he was to save the Jews.

Mordecai prayed and fasted for an answer to the decree, he told Ester what the king had planned to do and that she was also a Jew, that meant she would be killed also. He pleaded with her to go before the king and plead the case for the Jewish people. Now there was a law in the nation that anyone who came before the king without an invitation would be put to death, what was Ester to do, it seemed like her fate was sealed no matter what she done. Ester prayed to God for an answer and it came to her.

Ester put on her royal garments and was standing in the courtyard when king Xerxes looked out and noticed her, he asked her to join him and asked what he could do for her. She asked that he and Haman would come to a banquet that she would prepare for them the next day, he agreed and told Haman about her request, this made him very proud, he would be the only one there with the king and queen. As he left he ran into Mordecai, it still made him mad that he would not bow down to him so he ordered a gibbet to be erected, he was going to hang Mordecai.

That night the king couldn't go to sleep and he got up and started reading his court log and saw where Mordecai had informed him of the attempt to overthrow him, he asked the servant if anything was ever done for Mordecai to honor him and the servant said no. The guard heard something in the courtyard and asked who it was, Haman answered it was he, so the king invited him in. What should be done for the man whom the king wishes to reward? Haman thought he was talking about himself, so he told the king, you should place a royal robe on him and place him on the finest horse and parade him up and down the streets of the city saying, "this is what the king has done for the man whom the king wishes to reward." Xerxes told Haman that his idea was excellent and in the morning he wanted Haman to do exactly what he had proposed to do for Mordecai, so Haman did it and this angered him even more that he had to bestow such honors on a Jew.

The next day after the banquet the king asked Ester what he could do for her to show his gratitude. She asked him to spare her life and that of all her people. The king asked who was going to hurt her and she pointed to Haman, he had sent out a decree that all the Jews in the land of Persia was to be killed, Ester revealed to him that she was also a Jew, this angered the king and he had Haman hanged on the very gibbet that he had built for Mordecai. Now that Haman was gone the king appointed Mordecai in command and the Jewish nation flourished throughout the land.

There are many stories in the Bible of how God can take care of His children, it was not only in the days back then, He still watches over us today and He has our lives planned out for us. Our days were numbered before we were ever born, also He has a plan for our lives, but many times we do not follow His plan, that is why He gave each one of us a free will, we get to decide what road we want to go down. Sometimes the road we choose is not what He has planned but He still knows how to get us to our final destination if we will only trust Him and obey His laws. He only wants what is best for us, but sometimes He has to let us find out on our own, that is where all the heartaches and trials come from. If things aren't going the way you have planned maybe it's time you take another look at the roadmap, is there another way to get to your final destination? Do you even know where you want to go? Think about it and then decide!!!

EVERYONE HAS A NUMBER

Yes everybody has a number and every number will be called, sooner or later. It is a fact of life, we start dying when we are born. We start on our journey to our final destination, for some it is only a short time, for others it may be many years, but eventually everyone will close their eyes and breath their last breath. People try many things to try and prolong their life on Earth, but the cold hard fact is that one day we will meet our Creator. Some people don't even know who that is, some don't even care, they just live for now, never thinking about where they will spend Eternity or why they are even here to start with. Death, it sounds so final, many people are afraid to even think about it, they dread the day when they are going to face it, or maybe one of their family members, what they know about death is that every thing comes to an end. Your life is over.

But what if death was only the beginning, what if when you die you go to a Heavenly place where you will meet your Creator, would you still fear it so much? What if you know that when you breath your final breath here on Earth you will actually start to live a greater life. One that is filled with wonderful things, no more pain and sufferings, no sorrows or trials, wouldn't that be a place you would look forward too? I have really good news for you, Jesus, the Son of God came down upon this Earth, He conquered death. He died for our sins and took all our penalties and paid the price for us, He died so that we don't have to. Yes, we die leaving our human bodies behind, but our Spiritual Bodies live on for all Eternity, there in Heaven, a place created by God. The reason we are created in the first place is so we can be with God, He loves us so much that He wants us to be with Him forever. Jesus never came to Earth and died for us just so we can have a religion, He died for us because He loves us and wants to have a personal relationship with each one of us. Jesus tells us in the Bible that He is the Way, the Truth and the Life, that no one comes to the Father unless they come through Him, He is the only way!

We should not fear death, I know no one wants to die, that is our Human nature, to live as long as we can, to enjoy this life on Earth, but there is so much more waiting for us when we finally cross over. I read this saying in a book, "We are not Human beings, but Spiritual beings on a Human journey." One day our journey will be over, our number will be called. Where will you spend Eternity??

PSALMS 23, 5-6

YOU SPREAD THE TABLE BEFORE ME IN THE SIGHT OF MY FOES, YOU ANNOIT MY HEAD WITH OIL, MY CUP OVERFLOWS. ONLY GOODNESS AND KINDNESS SHALL FOLLOW ME ALL THE DAYS OF MY LIFE, AND I SHALL DWELL IN THE HOUSE OF THE LORD, FOR EVERMORE!!

A FACT OF LIFE

Have you ever accepted the fact, that one day you must die,
No one lives forever, this is the reason why.
We were created to be with God, to share in His infinite love,
In order to do so we must be cleansed, snow white, like a dove.
We choose Jesus Who gives us salvation, He Who is without sin,
He took our sins upon Himself, we start out spotless again.
We go through life we all make mistakes, but God sees only His Son,
And He forgives us, showers us with love, for all the wrongs we've done.
The fear of death is the greatest of fears, Satan uses this a lot,
He tries to steal our joy and happiness, but we must fear him not!
Cause Jesus triumphed over fear and death, He became our King,
Why should we fear meeting our Father, death, where is thy sting?
To those who are saved death has no grip, it's something everyone must
    do,
It's really the hardest on those left behind, people like me and you.
I feel for those who think life on Earth, is all that will ever be,
Death to them is a final act, they have nothing more to see.
But for us who know Jesus there is so much more, we will truly start to live,
To be with our Father and friends in heaven, isn't that why we forgive?
Don't mourn for me when my times comes, I'm ready to meet my Lord,
It's not the dying that I fear, it's the living that sometimes is hard!
Stay close to Jesus walk in His ways, do what He would have done,
When God looks down to see how we're doing, He'll see only His Son.
If you want this freedom that I possess, all you need do is ask,
Tell God you're sorry come in to my life, is that so great a task?
Then you will need not worry no matter what comes, Jesus will be in your
    heart,
And when you breathe that final breath, that's when your living will start!!

JOB

One day up in Heaven Satan appeared before God. God asked him what he had been doing and Satan answered he had been watching over the people on Earth. God asked him if he had noticed a man called Job. Satan answered yes he had and God asked him if he had noticed how obedient he was to which Satan replied that is very easy to be obedient when everything was going his way. What would happen to Job if some trials came his way, would he still continue to praise God, up to now Job had everything going his way. He had seven sons and three daughters and many cattle sheep and other animals, he was the richest man on Earth. So God told Satan that he could put Job to the test, he could do anything to Job but take his life, God knew that Job was a faithful servant.

So one day a servant came running to Job's house and told him that his enemy had come and stolen all his cattle and horses and killed all his herdsman, then another servant came and told him that lightening came down from the sky and killed all his sheep and the shepherds, he was the only one to escape. While they were still talking another came and told him that a big wind had come up and blew down the house where all his children where and that only he had escaped, they were all killed. Job tore his cloak and fell prostrate on the ground and said, "Naked I came into this world and naked I shall leave it, the Lord gave me everything and now He has taken it all away, but blessed be His Holy Name."

Now Satan came back very proud and told God to watch Job now that he had lost everything, but God showed Satan how Job was still praising His name. Satan told God that if He would only allow him to inflict some kind of pain on Job that he would surely curse God's name, so God allowed Satan to do whatever he wanted, but again he could not take his life.

So now Satan covered Job with boils, from his head to his toes, Job still did not curse the Lords name or say anything sinful. Jobs own wife told him to curse the name of the Lord and die, but he still believed God was in control and that He would again bless him.

Now that is what I would call patience and faith, Job believed in God no matter what came his way and God did reward him, He blessed him with greater riches than he had before. What are you believing God for, do you think He is capable of changing your life??

THE TEA CUP

Once their was this couple shopping in this little antique shop and they noticed this small tea cup up on the top shelf, it caught their eye and they both reached for it at the same time. They started laughing and Beth told her husband to go ahead and get it down. They liked it very much and thought it was very beautiful, they asked the store owner if he had any more like it and he said no. They were really surprised when the little cup began to speak to them, he told them that he wasn't always this beautiful, long ago he could remember when he was just a lump of clay and the master potter picked him up and began to squeeze him and shape him, it kind of hurt but there wasn't anything he could do about it. He placed the small cup on the wheel and it began to spin around and around, the potter began to shape the clay in the form of a cup and after he had finished he placed it on the shelf for a few days. Later he came back and he took me down and placed me in a very hot furnace, I thought I was going to burn up but I didn't, then he set me back up on the shelf. Later he came back and picked me up, he started covering me with some smelly paint, he let that dry for a few days, then he came back over and got me down again, he got out this pretty blue paint and he began to paint all these designs on me, I looked at myself in the mirror and I really liked what I saw, I was special, there wasn't anything around as pretty as me. He put me back up on the shelf for a few more days. When he came and got me he placed me back in the very hot furnace, I thought oh no, he is going to burn all the beautiful designs off of me that took him so long to paint, but once again, he knew what he was doing, instead the heat just hardened that paint and when he set me back up on the shelf I could see myself in the mirror, now I was even prettier than I had been, I had a shiny finish and everyone who came into his shop picked me up held me, they all thought I was very special, and I am.

Our Heavenly Father treats us this very same way, sometimes we have to go through some very trying times, we don't like it, but there isn't anything we can do, He knows by our trials we will grow and that one day we will get to see Him face to face. He has our lives planned out and if we follow His ways, we too will be very special, we will get to spend forever in Heaven!!

JUNKYARDS AND NURSING HOMES

The other day I was driving down this old road and I noticed this junkyard off to my left, I stopped and began to look it over to see if there were any old cars in it that I might be interested in. I walked around but nothing caught my eye so I drove off, it wasn't until later that I began to wonder about all those rusty cars and trucks, I had even saw an old r.v. and a camper, at some point everything here was once shiny and new, what kind of dreams did the people have who first bought them, what did they have to give up to purchase them, how did they change that persons life? So many times we live for the moment, we never think how something will change our lives in the years to come, we want something and we go after it. In some cases it may cost us our families, our friends, maybe even our lives. Would we still want that fast shiny new car if we knew that down the road that we would wreck it and be killed, wouldn't it be nice if we knew what the future held for us? Too many times we never think that far ahead, what kind of stories would we hear if those cars could talk, now they just set there rusting away, they are still worth something, but not much, there purpose has been fulfilled, what would they give to be shiny and new again, bringing laughter and joy to those who would ride in them once more.

I arrived at my destination, I was going to see a friend at the nursing home, she never had any family, only a few relatives that lived far away, but she did have a lot of friends who came and saw her. As I walked down the long hall that led to her room I noticed elderly people in wheelchairs, some were moving but others were asleep in them, they had started to go somewhere but got tired and just fell asleep. I had my visit with Anita and I left, as I made it back to the entrance I walked by some of the same people, they were in the same place, still sleeping away, nothing had changed. It wasn't until I drove away that I began to wonder if they had any family, they weren't always that old, what kind of life did they have, what kind of dreams did they have when they were young? Does anyone care about them now? Too many times we hear of stories where the kids just place their parents in the nursing homes and never come to see them, they are there, their purpose has been fulfilled, their lives are nearly over and their time is running short, but they still have a life.

God gives us all a chance, a chance to live with Him in Heaven, have you ever wondered what will happen to you when you get old and you are just living from day to day. Will you be like those rusty cars in the junkyard, hoping that someone will come along and make you new again, restore you. God has made us that promise, He tells us that we will be born again, that doesn't mean we will be born as a baby and have to go through this life again, it means we will have a new life in Heaven, with Him and all the people we know who has accepted Jesus as their Savior, we will all arise again, just like Jesus arose from the grave that very first Easter Sunday. We won't have this human body to get old and feel all the pain and go through all the sorrow, we will be Spiritual Beings, just like Jesus.

When I had my heart attack I thought that maybe my time had come and I would get to go to Heaven, but I guess it wasn't my time because I am still here, there is still something He wants me to do, maybe it is to help you to better understand what a Great God we have and that He wants all His children on Earth to be Saved.

You are not going to live forever, just visit a junkyard, a nursing home, or a cemetery. Life is very short compared to Eternity, where will you spend yours, 'SMOKING, OR NON-SMOKING'???

THE FROG

There was this old man, he was 85 and he decided to go fishing one morning. He hadn't caught anything and he heard someone say, "pick me up!" He looked around and didn't see anything, a few minutes later he heard it again, "pick me up", he looked around again and still he didn't see a thing, finally he looked down and he saw a frog setting there. The frog told him to pick her up and kiss her and she would turn into a beautiful young bride, he reached down and picked her up and looked at her and then he stuck her into his pocket. She said "hey wait, I told you to pick me up and kiss me and I would turn into a beautiful young bride," he just laughed and told her at his age he would rather have a frog that could talk!

This story reminds me of another old man in the bible, God spoke to him and told him that he and his wife was going to have a son and his descendents were going to be as numerous as the stars. Abraham was 99 years old and his wife was 90, so you can see why he would doubt that he and Sarah were going to have a son, but he had faith in his God and he knew that nothing was impossible with God.

After Isaac was born Abraham was again put to the test to see if he really trusted God and all that He told him to do. God told him to take his son and go up to the mountain and offer him up as a sacrifice, I don't believe many of us could pass this test, but he took him up and he built an alter and laid Isaac on it and was going to offer him up but God stopped him and told Abraham that now He knew he truly loved Him because he was willing to offer up his son as a sacrifice. God knew that later in time He was going to make the same choice when He had to give up His only Son Jesus as a sacrifice for the sins of all His children, that was the only way we could be made righteous in His sight. Since God was perfect, only a perfect sacrifice could atone for all our sins, when God looks at us, He doesn't see our sins, He sees the price paid as Jesus His Son laid down His life for all of us. Who else but a loving God could do this for all of us, do you know Him??

A POSITIVE ATTITUDE

Once there was a little five year old boy, his name was Joey. He had a very positive attitude at everything he did. One day as he was playing in his room he had the idea he could be the greatest batter there ever was, so he grabbed his bat and ball and went out into the back yard. He kept telling himself that he was the greatest batter there ever was and to prove it he was going to knock the ball out of the yard. He threw the ball up into the air and took a big swing and swish, nothing but air, strike one. So he reached down and picked up the ball and told himself again, I am the greatest batter there ever was, he tossed the ball up into the air and again, swish, nothing but air, strike two. He was beginning to lose just a little confidence but he said I can do this and again he told himself, I am the greatest batter there ever was, he reached down and picked up the ball, he took a deep breath and tossed the ball high into the air, he waited until just the right moment and he took a mighty swing, swish, nothing but air, strike three. Without missing a beat he reached down and picked up the ball and said wow, "I am the greatest pitcher there ever was!"

Everything in life is all about our attitude, we can choose to have a positive one, or we can choose to have a negative one, how we look at a situation is totally up to us. Some people take a negative situation and see only the bad or what went wrong, while others can have the same thing happen and look at it with a positive attitude, they can learn from what happened or use it to their advantage, it seems like life is never easy, there are difficulties every where we turn. How we let these trials affect us is dependant on how our attitude is in life. Try looking at everything with a positive attitude and see what a difference it will make, you might be surprised.

I read a phrase in a book the other day and I really think it is worth passing on. It said, "You can either be sorry the rosebush has thorns, or you can be thankful the thorn bush has roses!" How are you looking at the trials in your life, what kind of an attitude do you have?

2 TIMOTHY 1, 9-10

GOD HAS SAVED US AND HAS CALLED US TO A HOLY LIFE, NOT BECAUSE OF ANY MERIT OF OURS, BUT ACCORDING TO HIS OWN DESIGN. THE GRACE HELD OUT TO US IN CHRIST JESUS BEFORE THE WORLD BEGAN BUT NOW MADE MANIFEST THROUGH THE APPEARANCE OF OUR SAVIOR. HE HAS ROBBED DEATH OF ITS POWER AND HAS BROUGHT LIFE AND IMMORTALITY INTO CLEAR LIGHT THROUGH THE GOSPEL.

A REACHABLE JESUS

Sometimes in our frustration we say, "If God only knew what we are going
   through,"
But you see He does, He became a man like me and you.
The hands that healed the lepers, had dirt under the nails,
The feet that walked the Earth, traveled the dusty trails.
The tongue that told the parables, and healed the sick and dead,
The heart that felt the pain, at the accusations that were said.
The tears of joy, the tears of sadness, came from eyes that saw it all,
Because Jesus became a man like us, when He answered His Fathers call.
And people came to Him night and day, they pressed Him from every
   side,
Most did not believe in Him, no matter how hard He tried.
But there were those who saw the miracles, some were even healed,
Yet they cried, "CRUCIFY HIM", and His fate was sealed.
He could have come as a king on a royal throne, but He chose to come
   instead,
A touchable, reachable, human like us, a baby who had to be fed.
So He felt the pain, the hurt, the lies, He was let down by all His friends,
So God knows what we go through and He will be with us to the end.
So cast your cares upon our Father, He has been through it all before,
A lovable, reachable Jesus, waiting at the door!!

THE RED SHIRT

I heard a story about a young man, I'll call him Chris, he went to work for a construction company and he loved his job. Everyday he wore a red shirt, he went about doing his job, he was always willing to do anything the boss asked him to do. He was always ready to lend a helping hand to one of his fellow workers, it seemed he was always on the move and always in the right place at the right time. Every morning when the owner of the company came to the job site he would notice the red shirt, it seemed he was always busy doing something. After a few months passed the business grew and the owner was going to have to expand, he was going to make a new crew and he came out to the site to talk to the foreman, he wanted to get his opinion on who would make a good foreman for the new crew. As he pulled up he saw the red shirt, he didn't know the guys name but he remembered how every time he came out to the site this guy was always busy so he asked the foreman who he was and told him of his plan. The foreman said, yeah that is Chris, he is a very good worker, it seems he is always willing to help out, he gets along good with everyone on the site, I guess its that red shirt he always wears, it seems like he is every where. He got the new job!

As you go through life you are always given a choice, you can choose to be just like everyone else, or you can choose to be just a little better, go the extra mile, excel in the task you are given to do. As long as your attitude is, I do just as much as the next guy, you will probably always be just an ordinary person doing an ordinary job. It is when you try just a little harder, go just a little farther, care just a little more, willing to make a difference, help others along the way, that is when you will get ahead. Try it and see if it will work for you, you may be surprised. At first you may be made fun of or called names, it seems like those around you want to keep you in the same boat, sometimes you have to get out of the boat, take a step of faith and oh yeah, it may not hurt to wear a red shirt!!!

WHY DOES GOD ALLOW TRIALS IN OUR LIVES

When we receive Jesus and are saved, the Holy Spirit comes and lives inside us, we become filled with the Spirit. Since none of us are perfect we sin, when we sin we can either be sorry for our sins, or we can try and convince ourselves that what we did was not a sin, we try to cover it up. Since God loves us so much, He tries to make us see the errors of our ways. He first tries to convict us, He lets us know that what we are doing is wrong, but when we have sinned and His conviction doesn't work on us because we have hardened our hearts or tried covering up our sin He has to try another way. He loves us too much to just let us keep on sinning, so He has to get our attention somehow, so He allows trials to come into our lives. They may be just small things at first, something that may cause us to question why these things are happening to me? But if that doesn't work He may try other things, how sensitive are you to His convictions? How far will God have to go to get your attention?

I know when I sin I don't always recognize it right away, sometimes I try to cover it up, I try to make excuses, I try to say everyone else is getting by with it, but then the conviction comes. I am not everyone else. What other people do is not what I am being judged on, it is what I do and say, God only judges us on what we do, we will only have to answer for our actions. Since He loves me so much He is not going to let me stay out of His will, He has my life planned out and He only wants what is best for me, so if I begin to wander from the narrow path He has prepared for me He has ways to get my attention. He tries the conviction thing, but if that doesn't work He has other ways to get it. When I know things in my life seem to be getting just a little more complicated I know He is dealing with me about something, I have to just get back in touch with Him and find out where I am going wrong. Only you will know where you are going astray. The big question is, what will it take to get you back on track?

God has no eraser on His pencil, once your name is written in the book of life He will do whatever He has too to get your attention, it is up to you how far He needs to go. God loves us so much He gave up His only Son to die for us, do you think He will give up on you. Trials may come, but they are only a way to get our attention!!

HOW FAR WILL A FATHER GO

I heard a story about a native Indian tribe that lived by the Niagra Falls, every year they would make a sacrifice of a young virgin from the tribe to the Spirit of the Mighty river. She was called the "Bride of the Falls." They would load a canoe with the very best of their produce and some of their most valued possessions and then they would place this virgin in the canoe, take her out in the strong current and she would drift to the Falls and go over, to her final resting grounds.

This old chief was sitting in his teepee one day when they brought him the news that his only daughter was chosen to be the Bride. He never said a word, he just kept smoking his pipe, everyone thought he would surely stop the sacrifice, he made no remarks. When the day finally came the canoe was prepared and the Bride was placed in it, they took her out to the middle of the river and let her go, as she started drifting towards the Falls they saw this other canoe come out into the river, it was the old chief. He paddled as fast as he could and he came along side of the canoe that held his daughter, as the two embraced she could see the love in her fathers eyes and she knew she would not go through this alone, her father was there by her side as they both went over the falls and too their death.

You may not know this, but our Heavenly Father has that same kind of love for every one of His children, He doesn't want any one of us to parish, He loves us so much that He actually came down upon this Earth and suffered and died for our sins. He died and rose again to Heaven to show us that love. He shows us there is more to this life than just the life we live here on Earth. When He created us He gave us a body and a Spirit, the Spirit lives on for all Eternity and one day we will stand and be judged for the way we chose to live while we were here on Earth, the good news is that if we accept Jesus as our Savior and we are sorry for our sins we won't be judged by what we have done, our Father will only see the sacrifice His Son made for us and we will join Them in Heaven. How far will a Father go to prove His love for us? ALL THE WAY!!!!

THE BLUE DRESS

I heard a story about this lady who had a big problem with her credit cards, she was always charging them up and her husband was on her all the time about it. One day she told her husband she would not do it any more and gave him her word. Not long after that she was walking down the street and she saw this beautiful blue dress in the stores window, she had this thought, it wouldn't hurt anything if I just went in and tried it on, so she did. She just couldn't resist, it looked so good on her so she charged it. Later that evening she walked into the house and her husband saw the box under her arm and began to question her, she told him how she was just going to try it on and how good it looked on her so she had to have it. He told her that this was just a trick of the devils, he told her that she should have told the devil, "Get thee behind me Satan!" She said I did, that's when he told me, "It looks even better from behind!"

Many times the devil uses little thoughts to get into your mind, maybe it's like, no one will notice this one time, you can do it once and get by with it, everyone else is doing it. He comes at you from all directions, he tries to convince you that what you are about to do is ok, this once becomes a habit and sometimes bad habits are hard to break. You have this little small voice inside you that only you can hear, it's a gut feeling, you know when something is wrong or it just doesn't feel right, but you go ahead and do it anyway, many times we regret the action we took but it is too late, now you have to live with your actions. Have you ever been there or done that? Most people if they are honest with themselves will say yeah, I have had that feeling or heard that still small voice but I wanted to do it anyway, that is where we all get into trouble. Make a pact with yourself, the next time you feel uneasy about something, stop, think it over, think about how this action will affect your life. That blue dress, or shiny car, or good time may be just one of the little tricks the devil has up his sleeve to get you into some kind of situation that may be hard to get out of. DIRECTION, NOT INTENTION, DETERMINES OUR DESTINATION!!!

THE PRODIGAL FATHER

Once upon a time there was this family, the young couple had 2 sons, the father loved his family very much but he had one drawback. He loved his job more! As the two sons began to grow up they missed all the things that other sons got to do with their father, he was always busy at work. One day they got together and agreed on a plan, they would ask their father for their allotment of time from their father. He agreed and for a whole month he would do anything that the two boys wanted to do. They went fishing, camping, to baseball games, they went to the theme parks and rode all the rides, they had a blast doing all the things with their father that they had heard other kids just talk about. The month was over before the boys could do all the things they had hoped to do and now dad had to go back to work, he really enjoyed his time with the boys, in fact he had a great time and he wished he could do this more often but he had bills to pay and was putting away for the boys to go to college, he wanted them to attend the finest schools, he had such high hopes for his sons, he wanted them to have all the things he never had when he was growing up, all he could think of was making more money so that one day they could have the life he dreamed of and wanted to give them.

Years went by and the sons left for college, neither son wanted to go but they went just so their father would be happy. While they were there they got in with the wrong crowd and got hooked on drugs and just made a mess of their life. Their father was too busy making money to even notice what was happening to their lives, he was now the boss at his company and things were going very well for him. He had climbed the corporate ladder at the expense of his family, he never even noticed all the time that had slipped away, it now came time for him to retire, he thought at last, now we can do all the things that he had only dreamed of when he was a young man. Only one thing, now the boys were grown, they had their own family, he never took time to be with them when they were young, he missed their whole life, he never enjoyed any time with them, except for that one month way back when. He went back to that month time and again and tried to bring back those memories but the time had faded them out, now he would give all the money that he had ever made if he could just spend time with his family.

He had an idea, he would call his sons and ask them over and they could start over, he could give them everything that they wanted. He picked up the phone and called but the boys couldn't make it, they had things to do and places to go, they had their lives to live and since he never took the time to be with them they made excuses every time he called. All he had was his money, his wife had died a few years back, he remembered the boys coming to the funeral with their families, he couldn't even remember his grand children's names, what a mess he had made of his life.

He got on a plane and went out to the town where the two sons had moved too, he thought if I just go to them they will see how much I really care for them. He never called or told them he was coming, one day he just showed up, as he went up to each of them he thought it may be like the story of the Prodigal Son that his Sunday school teacher had taught him so many years ago, it wasn't, neither of the boys welcomed him, he only had himself to blame, he never cared about their wants when they were little and needed him, now they didn't need him. He had money, he had time, but he didn't have a family, do you know someone like this? Maybe this is you!! Don't let money and power take control of your life, there is so much more, you can never replace the time you spend doing whatever it is you do.

Make the time you have count and be the person you dream right now because we are not going to be here forever and time slips away before you know it and sometimes it is too late, sometimes you can't replace the time you lost. Sometimes time is more important than money, don't be like the Prodigal Father!!!

DEUTERONOMY 31 : 6

I AM STRONG AND OF GOOD COURAGE, I DO NOT FEAR NOR AM I AFRAID, FOR THE LORD MY GOD, HE IS THE ONE GOES WITH ME. HE WILL NOT LEAVE ME NOR FORSAKE ME.

YOUR WILL

Father You led me into the wilderness, when I had lost my way,
You showed me the peace and joy of heaven, now I'm here to stay.
I don't know where my journey will lead, my life has ups and downs,
But I know for sure when my life is through, You'll reward me with a
    crown.
I once was lost but now I've found, Your love I can't replace,
It keeps me going every day, till I look upon Your Face.
I trusted You when all hope was gone, and I had no place to turn,
You never let me walk alone, this I had to learn.
You led me down life's narrow paths, sometimes I didn't follow,
But You never did give up on me, nor fill my life with sorrow.
You gave me strength to carry on, even when I turned my back,
You always had someone special, to get me back on track.
So now I give my life to you, mold me like I was clay,
Put in my heart and mind and soul, the words You want me to say.
For Jesus Your Son has died for me, He took my place my sin,
He opened the gates of heaven, and invites all to come in!
He paid the price, once for all, He became the perfect Lamb,
Not everyone will accept His gift, but you can be sure I am.
So thank You Father for the gifts You gave, my life has been a thrill,
I give You praise, I give You glory, as I carry out Your will!!

THE NARROW PATH

This is a story about a young man, let's call him Chris, he was just like most ordinary young men, he came from an ordinary family. He went to church and had a very good life. When he was in high school all his friends went to a different church than where he was brought up and he wanted to go to that church, his parents agreed as long as he went to church it was fine with them. He enjoyed singing in the choir because all his friends did, he had a very good voice, later he even joined their church and accepted Jesus as his Savior and was Baptized. He finished high school and went to college, there, one of his friends got him a job, singing in the choir at a church nearby, now he was doing something he really liked and was even being paid for it! This went on all through college and he even did it for a short while after he graduated. When he was out of school he tried several places to get a job, not much success though. While he was in college he drifted away from church, he still sang at the church where he was getting paid but it wasn't the same, he was doing it for the money, not to praise the Lord and worship Him, maybe that's why when he went to try and get a job he never had much success. I have always heard if God be for you, who can be against you, it seems like something or some one was against him because nothing ever seemed to go right, things broke down, couldn't land a real good job, life in general just wasn't as much fun as it used to be. Could it be that he had wandered off the narrow path and God was trying to get him back on, I guess he never thought of it that way because he never has gone back to church or tried putting God first in his life again. I have always heard that once you are saved God will use any method to get you back on the straight and narrow path, for some it just takes longer and even a little more hardship, God will allow bad situations to happen in peoples lives to get them back where they need to be. Have you ever noticed this in your life, I have! The story of Chris is still being played out, how long it takes him to surrender his will to God is up to him, only he can choose the path he wants to walk, each one of us has our own life and we are the only ones who choose which road we will go down, I hope yours is always smooth and straight and has God leading your way, for if He be for us, who can be against us???

ICE CREAM IS GOOD FOR THE SOUL

There was this family who came into this café to eat one day and after they had ordered their food the six year old son asked his dad if he could say grace. The father said you sure can and the young boy began, "God is great, God is good, thank you Father for this food. Help us in our life today and help us with what we do and say. And oh yeah, it would be nice if dad bought us some ice cream, thanks!"

After he got done these two old ladies setting at the next table began talking about how this dad could allow his son to pray to God that way, the little boy heard them and asked his dad if God was mad at him. His dad told him no that God wasn't mad at him, God enjoyed hearing from all his children and his prayer was just fine. It was then that an old man stopped by their table and commented on the boys prayer, he said it was very thoughtful and God loved him and that ice cream was good for his soul.

After they had finished eating dad bought a round of ice cream and as the waitress brought it to the table and set it down before them the young boy looked up and said, "Thank you Father," then he picked up his bowl of ice cream and gave it to the old ladies and told them that his soul was good and that they needed it more than he did!!

How many times do we act religious and pious, wanting everyone around to see us, to know that we are Christians, but are we really? I think sometimes we take it a little too far, we think everything has to be all churchy and reverent. We try to impress others but we should really be trying to show others that God loves us no matter what, He made us and He only wants what is best for us, He sees everything we do and He knows our heart. That little boy was a good example how we should approach our Heavenly Father, we should adore Him, give Him thanks and if we have a request, bring it to His attention, He is always listening. Have you requested your bowl of ice cream lately?

THE TRAIL

A family went camping one day and when they got to the campground they began to unpack. The dad pitched the tent and gathered some rocks and was going to make a campfire, he looked everywhere for the lighter fluid, he thought he had gotten some but it was no where to be found. He still had some more to do at the campsite so he asked his young son if he could run down to the store and pick him up a can, it was just a short way down the hill and there was a path all the way down to the store since many campers used it to go and get things they had forgotten or needed.

At first Johnny was afraid he might get lost but his dad assured him if he just followed the path he would make it there and back just fine, he brought him to the edge of camp and pointed to a big pine tree off in the distance, you see that tree Johnny, the path goes right beside it. Johnny started down the path and when he got to the tree he looked down the path and he saw another big tree, so he walked to that one, from there he could see the store off in the distance. He went inside, got the lighter fluid and started back to the campsite, when he got back on the path he wasn't afraid any more because he knew it would lead him back to his family.

God has a path for each one of us to follow also, we never know what lies ahead or around the next corner but He is always with us and He is willing to help us anytime we ask Him too. If you don't know God you can find out about Him by reading books or talking to people who go to church, most are willing to share their love of God with you, He is Someone that will make a real difference in your life. He has this place called Heaven waiting for all His children, all we have to do is accept Jesus His Son as our Savior and follow the trail He has laid out for us because He came down to Earth and suffered and died for our sins. Just like Johnny, once we accept Jesus into our lives we won't be afraid anymore!

I know not when or where I go, from this familiar place,
But He is here and He is there, and I will look upon His face.
And when I pass from all I know to a life that is unknown,
Though longer I stay, or soon I go, I shall not go alone!!!

If you knew that tomorrow would be your last day on Earth would you do anything different today? Would you take time to make up with someone that you can't get along with, maybe you are ends with one of your children or a family member. How would you like the world to remember you? Is there something you would like to tell those you love so they wouldn't make the same mistakes that you have made. Life is so short compared to Eternity, have you given any thought to where you are going to spend Eternity, will it make a difference? So many questions and so short a time to find out the answers. We don't have that luxury of knowing when we are going to breath our last breath, the hands of time keep ticking away and no one knows when they will finally stop. If you could know for certain that you would go to Heaven wouldn't that be a comforting thought for you and for all those you love. There is a way you know, just ask Jesus to come into your life and be sorry for all the wrongs you have ever done, nothing will keep you from your Heavenly Father if you would just take the time to ask Jesus to come into your heart. Look at the thief who was crucified with Jesus, no one knows how bad he lived up until that day, but dying on the cross there on Calvary with Jesus at his side he asked Jesus to remember him when he got to heaven and Jesus told him that this day, he would be in Heaven with Him. What a wonderful feeling he must have had, knowing that he was on his way to Heaven to spend Eternity with God. You can be certain also, the choice is yours, won't you make your choice today, tomorrow may be too late!!

MIKE